FAMILIES

by Meredith Tax

Illustrated by Marylin Hafner

The Feminist Press
at The City University of New York
New York

Published by The Feminist Press at The City University of New York
365 Fifth Avenue, New York, NY 10016

First Feminist press edition, 1996

05 04   8 7 6 5 4

Library of Congress Cataloging-in-Publication Data

Tax, Meredith
    Families / by Meredith Tax : illustrated by Marylin Hafner
        p.   cm.
    Originally published: Boston : Little, Brown, © 1981.
        Summary: Describes different kinds of families.
    ISBN: 1-55861-157-6 (pbk: alk. paper)
    1. Family — United States — Juvenile Literature
    [1. Family.] I. Hafner, Marylin, ill.   II. Title.
    HQ536 .T39 1996   96-15998
    306.85—dc20   CIP
                                             AC

This publication is made possible, in part, by public funds from the New York State Council on the Arts. The Feminist Press would like to thank Helene D. Goldfarb, Joanne Markell, Rubie Saunders, Barbara Smith, Caroline Urvater, and Genevieve Vaughan for their generosity.

Cover and interior watercolor by Cathy Ascienzo

Printed in Mexico by
R. R. Donnelley and Sons, Inc.

To Corey and her friends at P.S. 75

— M. T.

For Nanny and Dave, family, too

— M. H.

My name is Angie. I am six. Here is everything I know about families.

Families are who you live with and who you love. I live with my mother most of the time and with my father on vacations. I also have two grandmas and one grandpa and some aunts and uncles and cousins. They are all in my family, but I don't live with them.

My mother and I live in a big building in New York. We have a laundry in the basement. I help to do the wash: I carry the soap and put the money in the slot and fold the dry clothes. Then my mother says, "Thank you, partner," and kisses my nose.

My father lives in Boston with my stepmother, Alice. They have a little baby named Mickey. He's my half brother. We have the same father but not the same mother so he's only a half, but he's just as good as a whole.

I help burp him after he has his bottle. The burp sounds as loud as a firecracker and makes me laugh. Then Mickey smiles too. My father says it's because his stomach feels better, but I think it's because he's glad I'm there.

This is a lion's family: one father, one mother, and three cubs. They all live together in a cage at the zoo. My friend George also lives with one father, one mother, and two brothers — but not in a cage.

His big brother, Gus, is nine. Sometimes he lets us play baseball with him, but we never get to bat. I'm the catcher. George says that when his baby brother can walk he'll let him be the catcher, then I can pitch and George will be the batter. I say we should all share.

This is my friend Marisol from school. She has a big family. She lives with her mother, her Aunt Rosa, her grandma and grandpa, her brothers, Carlos and Hector, and her baby sister, Mariana. Her father and another grandma live in Puerto Rico. Marisol's Aunt Rosa works in a dress factory. She is very good at making clothes, and made Marisol a pink party dress for her birthday.

When I went to Marisol's party, her Aunt Rosa looked at the label in my dress and started to laugh. She said she made my dress too, when she was at work! I said, "It's a good thing you did or I wouldn't have anything to wear."

Marisol taught me to say hello in Spanish.

This is my cousin Louie. He's adopted. That means he didn't come from my Aunt Julie's belly, but they got him someplace else. They get to keep him forever, though. Louie is very tough. He broke his arm falling out of a tree and only cried a little. Aunt Julie says she loves every bone in his body and hopes he doesn't break them all before he's ten.

These are ants. They live in a glass box in my school. There is only one mother ant, the queen, but lots of fathers and hundreds and hundreds of tiny babies. You can hardly see them, they're so small. When I was little I used to step on ants, but now I don't because their families might be sad.

Douglas has two beds! One is at his mother's and the other is downstairs at his grandma's. He stays downstairs during the week because his mother works nights managing a bakery and his grandma brings him to school in the morning.

On weekends he stays with his mom, and she takes him to the playground and brings a big bag of donuts from her job and gives them to all the kids. I like Douglas's mother.

This is my mom's friend Emma. She lives with Arthur. They have no kids, but they like them to visit. They have a collection of sixteen paperweights with snow falling inside, and they let me play with them. I try to make them all snow at once.

Here is a family of chickens. They live together in a chicken coop.
There are lots of mother hens, but only one father for all these baby
chicks. He's a rooster.

Willie lives with his father. He knows how to sew on Willie's buttons when they come off, and he makes him pancakes and bacon every Sunday morning. He invited our whole class on Willie's birthday — twenty-five kids! My mother said, "You've got to be kidding," but

he said, "You're only five once." There was a great big cake with super-heroes all over it because Willie wants to be a superhero when he grows up. All the other parents helped clean up after the party because it got a little messy.

Susie lives with her mother and her godmother. They took her to the roller rink and she won a prize for the best skater under twelve. The prize was a silver pin shaped like a roller skate. When I asked Susie where her father lives, she said she doesn't have any father.

So George said he would be her father. Then Douglas said he wanted to be her father too, so we had to let them both do it. Susie was the baby and Willie was the brother and Marisol was the mother. I got to be the teacher. Kids can be like families too.

Some dogs have people for a family. They only live with their own mothers when they are babies; after that they move out and live with people. But when they see other dogs in the street, they are very interested. A woman in our building has four dogs, but I don't think they are brothers because they look so different.

Sometimes I wish my parents both lived in one house like George's, or at least in the same city. But he wants to be like me. He asked his mom when she was going to get a divorce because he wants to fly to Boston all by himself. "It's not fair," he told me. So I said he could come with me if he lets me ride his bike whenever I want.

There are lots of different kinds of families. Some are big and some are small. Some are animals and some are people. Some live in one house and some live in two or three.

The main thing isn't where they live or how big they are —

it's how much they love each other.

Titles in the Series

FUN TIME
HAPPY DAYS
FAVORITE TOYS
BEST OF FRIENDS
ROCKY'S BIG SURPRISE
PARTY TIME
CAMPING OUT
TIGER'S SPECIAL DAY

Sunshine Books™ is a trademark owned
by Modern Publishing, A Division of
Unisystems, Inc.
© 1986 Text Copyright by Joshua Morris, Inc.
© 1986 Illustrations Copyright by Hemma.
All rights reserved.
Printed in Singapore

ROCKY'S
BIG SURPRISE

ILLUSTRATED BY RUTH MOREHEAD
TEXT ADAPTED BY GWEN MONTGOMERY

Modern Publishing
A Division of Unisystems, Inc.
New York, New York 10022

One afternoon, Rocky Rabbit went to visit his friends, Rusty and Tiger. "Stay for dinner," said Rusty. "We'll make grandma's vegetable soup." Rocky was happy. He loved vegetable soup.

Rusty decided to look up the soup recipe in grandma's old cookbook. "Let's see, vegetable soup has potatoes, onions, and ... Oh no, a page is missing! What should I do? I know! I'll go to the garden. Maybe I'll remember while I pick some vegetables."

Rocky and Tiger wanted to help too. "We'll all go and pick vegetables," they cried. Rocky carried the shovel. Tiger carefully carried the clipping shears. And Rusty carried the big wicker basket.

Rocky liked working in the garden. He could daydream while he worked, and pretend to be anything he wanted. Digging in the garden made him think of a treasure hunt. "If I dig deep enough," he thought to himself, "I might find a buried treasure!"

Rocky dug and dug. But he didn't find
buried treasure. "Nothing here but the
vegetables for vegetable soup," he sighed,
and tossed the potatoes and onions in the
air. "But these are fun to juggle. Hey! Maybe
I should join the circus!" Rocky tossed the
vegetables around and around.

Soon Tiger grew tired of picking vegetables. "I'll take a little catnap right here," he said, curling into a little ball. But suddenly, he felt something tickling his nose.

"No sleeping on the job!" laughed Rusty. And he tickled Tiger with the celery.

Tiger looked at all the vegetables. "We need our wagon," he said. When he returned, Rocky, Rusty and Tiger loaded the wagon with all the vegetables.

"There's still something missing from our soup," said Rusty. "I wish I could remember what it is."

Suddenly, Rocky shouted, "I know what the soup is missing. And I know just where I can find it. I'll be right back with a special surprise!" And off he ran.

"I wonder what Rocky's special surprise could be?" Tiger asked.

"I don't know," said Rusty. "But we need to get the fire started for the soup. I'd better gather fire wood right now!"

Rusty ran into the forest and gathered as much wood as he could find.

Meanwhile, Rocky had gone back to his own little garden. "Carrots!" he exclaimed happily. "Vegetable soup isn't soup without carrots." He ate a few carrots right there, and took the rest back to Rusty and Tiger's house.

When Rocky returned, Rocky put his surprise in the kitchen. Tiger had just put the wood in the fireplace. "Let's start the fire now, " said Tiger. But no matter how hard Tiger and Rocky tried, they couldn't light the fire.

Tiger climbed up to the roof. "Maybe something's wrong with the chimney," he thought. "Mrs. Stork!" cried Tiger. "The chimney is not a very good place for a nest!"

"Indeed!" snorted Mrs. Stork. "I'm moving to a nice safe tree!" and she flew away carrying her nest.

Soon the fire started. "I'll help carry the kettle to the fireplace," said Rocky. "I'll pretend I'm a soldier. One, Two, Three, Four … One, Two, Three, Four!" Rocky and Rusty marched around the room.

"Time to start the soup!" said Tiger, running back into the house. Rusty and Tiger went into the kitchen. And there on the table was Rocky's special surprise.

"Carrots!" said Rusty and Tiger in surprise. "That's what was missing!"

When the soup was ready, they all sat down to eat. "Mmm," said Rocky, taking a sip. "This is the best soup I've ever had!"

"Yes," said Rusty laughing, "Now we know that friendship is what makes this vegetable soup so special!" And the three friends ate and ate, until the soup was all gone!